MW01155014

Art for the
Traditional Home

A Collection of Frameable, *Original Prints* from Top Artists

One-of-a-kind artwork *expertly* curated by

Ashley *and* Jamin Mills

The Handmade Home:
Creating a Haven for the Every Day

thehand
madehome
.net

Aadamsmedia
Avon, Massachusetts

Published by
Adams Media, a division of F+W Media, Inc.
57 Littlefield Street, Avon, MA 02322. U.S.A.
www.adamsmedia.com

ISBN 10: 1-4405-7088-4
ISBN 13: 978-1-4405-7088-9

Printed in Mexico.

10 9 8 7 6 5 4 3 2 1

Many of the designations used by manufacturers and sellers to distinguish their product are claimed as trademarks. Where those designations appear in this book and F+W Media was aware of a trademark claim, the designations have been printed with initial capital letters.

Cover images © Annie Bailey, David Scheirer, Amy Tyler, Grapefruit Design, Sarah B. Martinez, Sonja Caldwell.

This book is available at quantity discounts for bulk purchases.
For information, please call 1-800-289-0963.

Introduction

When you choose something for your home that you truly adore, it speaks to you. It moves you; it sparks something almost inexplicable in your soul. In the search for that gem, you create timeless spaces that tell the story of your life. By juxtaposing items that flow together in your own style, you become the ultimate composer of your spaces.

Now, with the forty inspiring pieces of art found within *The Custom Art Collection: Art for the Traditional Home*, you'll be able to quickly and easily find that perfect addition to your space; that much-needed, one-of-a-kind creation! This carefully curated, eclectic array of

inspiring pieces you'll find throughout are all from incredibly talented photographers, designers, and artists we love. With their participation and generosity, we are able to showcase a glimpse of their creations. Just for you!

Now that you've found pieces that you love, what next? The prints included here will fit any 8" × 10" frame, with limitless possibilities for matting and frame design. The perforated edge makes it easy to remove the images and create your own art gallery in just minutes!

When it comes to using art in your home, there are a lot of different opinions out there, and sometimes all those voices can be a little overwhelming. We believe, first and foremost, that you should do what feels right to you. But what do you do when in doubt? Here are three main categories we stick to when it comes to grouping art.

1. Color

- **Create Depth:** Use pieces that have varying shades in the same tones to create depth and interest on your walls. Consider this strategy with both frames and art. The frames are just as important, so let them work together to hold something beautiful on those walls.

- **Play with Contrast:** Think in terms of opposites and try to balance them. Bringing in an element like a metal frame and juxtaposing it with natural wood, or traditional art with contemporary can create a beautiful look all on its own.

- **Freshen Up:** When searching for the perfect frames to group together, don't forget to scout sales racks at home design stores for interesting shapes. Or even try shopping the rooms of your own home for a new spin on a forgotten piece. You can bring new life to old frames by unifying them with varying shades of the same color. This applies to the matte in a frame, too. Don't let a blah color hold you back. Give it a spritz with spray paint; add stripes with painter's tape; or use a stencil for a bold, unexpected statement.

2. Numbers

- **Odd Numbers:** When dealing with groupings, odd numbers are known to play with the eye to create a more appealing display.

- **Even Numbers:** If you prefer symmetry on your walls, try even-numbered groupings. Always use pairings or equal numbers when going for a bold, simplistic statement, and a cleaner look.

- **Ratio:** When using frames together, remember this: One large frame paired with two smaller ones makes a great balanced look, even when working with odd numbers. Always consider this element in your groupings.

3. Display

- **Always at Eye Level:** The most common mistake we see is hanging art too high. Strive for eye level. When hanging frames in groups, always go for a spacing that keeps them closer, with the negative space greater on the outsides than in between.
- **Hanging over Furniture:** Keep frames and art no higher than 5 to 6 inches above a piece of furniture for a clean, intentional look.
- **Practice Makes Perfect:** Hanging things on the wall can sometimes feel laborious and downright intimidating. Don't be afraid to sketch it out for proportions, lay it on the floor, and measure. Cut pieces of paper to size and tape them to the wall to try it out. Ask your friends for another opinion. Small holes in walls are pretty forgiving in the grand scheme of things, so even if you mess up, there's a fix for that.

Above all, be brave, stay flexible, and just go for it. This is how we grow, learn, and create personal displays of beautiful, one-of-a-kind art in our homes!

It is our hope that, within the pages of this book, you find inspiration. If you're looking for your voice or maybe even a springboard to cultivate your home into a reflection of who you really are, we hope that you find something you're crazy about, let go of your fears, and love the home you create. And if you're looking for more design options or need help arranging these beautiful images, take a look at *Handmade Walls*, *The Custom Art Collection: Art for the Contemporary Home*, and *The Custom Art Collection: Art for the Eclectic Home*, the companions to this title.

The walls of your home hold the potential for great beauty and we hope you feel passionate about the possibilities for beauty that lie within. After all, when you add something that speaks to you, it truly can take your space to an entirely different level of amazing. Art is the perfect place to begin . . . the ultimate inspiration.

Ashley *and* Jamin Mills
The Handmade Home:
Creating a Haven for the Every Day

thehand
madehome
.net

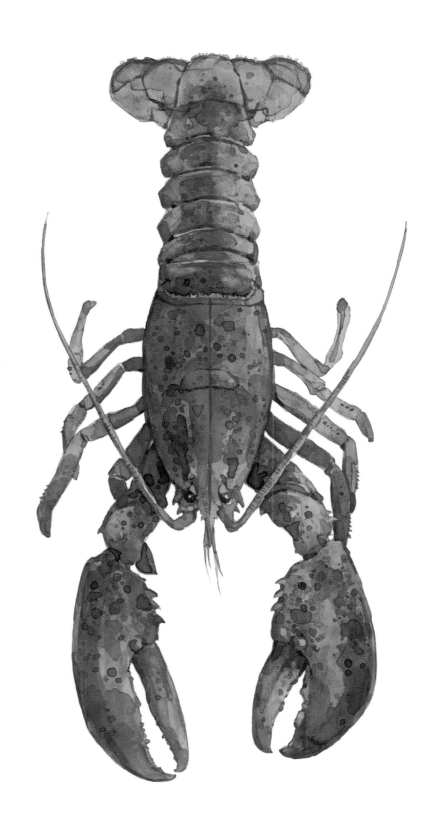

David Scheirer
"Red Lobster"

Ashley Mills
"Vintage Americana—Interior"

Miriam Schulman
"Yasgur's Farm"

Patricia Cotterill
"Underwood Typewriter"

Sonja Caldwell
"Portofino"

Rachel Perkos 06

Rachel Parker
"Silver Polish"

Amy Tyler
"Torch Song"

Ashley Mills
"In Flight"

Annie Bailey
"First to Turn"

Amy Tyler
"Sweet Rides"

Brandy Cattoor
"Eggs in a Basket"

Annie Bailey
"Happy Accidents"

Ashley Mills
"Vintage Americana—Rest"

Ashley Mills
"Vintage Americana—Rusted"

Patricia Cotterill
"Piano Keys"

David Scheirer
"Lobster Buoys"

Bree Madden
"Hanalei Bay"

Bree Madden
"Golden Gate Bridge"

Carolyn Finnell
"Hide and Seek"

I LOVE YOU

A BUSHEL & A PECK

YOU BET YOUR PURDY NECK I DO

Emily Jones
"Bushel & a Peck"

do not worry

about

TOMORROW

for tomorrow will worry about itself

Emily Jones
"Do Not Worry about Tomorrow"

David Scheirer
"Curtis Island Lighthouse"

Marianne LoMonaco
"Blackberries"

Michelle Tavares
"Poppies"

Larisa Brechun
"Grapes"

Patricia Cotterill
"Moo"

Ammonitida

Grapefruit Design
"The Grey Amonitida"

Rachel Parker
"Covering Ground"

David Scheirer
"8 Quail Eggs"

Larisa Brechun
"Cherries"

Rachel Parker

Rachel Parker
"Sunday Hydrangeas"

Credits

Jonathan Aller
"Evening Tea"
www.JonAllerPaintings.com
Jonathan Aller spent most of his life sketching everything he sees. His passion for sketching and drawing carried into a love for painting. After graduating from Ringling College of Art and Design, he traveled to Florence, Italy and studied at the Angel Academy Atelier. There, he was taught the techniques of the masters. Having been exposed to so many artists, he gained an even deeper respect for painting and its history.

Annie Bailey, *Montana Photo Journal*
"First To Turn"
"Happy Accidents"
www.MTPhotoJournal.Etsy.com
Annie Bailey is the photographer for Montana Photo Journal. Her work is a reflection of a life spent surrounded by open space and blue sky. She was born and raised in Montana, with most of her life spent on her family's ranch in the Smith River valley. Seeing and documenting the tiny moments in life is what she wants to do for the rest of her life.

Larisa Brechun
"Grapes"
"Cherries"
Born and raised in Birmingham, Alabama, Larisa Brechun has always enjoyed all types of art. Five years ago, she experimented with oil paints and discovered it to be the perfect medium for her. She enjoys painting a variety of subjects. Her work can be seen at Littlehouse Galleries in Homewood, Alabama.

Sonja Caldwell
"Portofino"
SonjaCaldwell.Etsy.com
Sonja was born in Kansas but moved to Japan at age 7, then to California at age 10. She holds a BA in studio art

from UC Davis. Being the daughter of a wanderlust and an international businessman, she has always enjoyed travel photography and has had a lot of opportunities to do it. As a photographer, her main subject is Paris, France. She splits her time between Paris and her home in San Jose, California.

Brandy Cattoor
"Eggs in a Basket"
www.BrandyCattoor.com
Brandy Cattoor graduated with a BFA in oil painting from Brigham Young University Idaho in 2011. She has completed commission work for drawings and oil paintings. She is interested in architectural landscapes, cityscapes, still lifes, and portraiture. Along with oil painting, Brandy creates and sells handmade paper products. Eventually she hopes to merge both creative forms into one.

Grapefruit Design
"Natural Mandalas"
"Turquoise Octopus"
"The Grey Amonitida"
www.SeasidePrint.Etsy.com
Living on the coast, it was not unthinkable that Magalí and Gabi would end up with Seaside Prints. Together, they run three online shops of prints and posters. The shops allow them to dig into antique and vintage ephemera in search of inspiration; they also keep them really busy!

Patricia Cotterill
"Piano Keys"
"Underwood Typewriter"
"Moo"
PCotterill.Etsy.com
Born in Scotland, Patricia Cotterill lived in Europe, the Middle East and Asia before settling in Asheville, NC. This has left a deep impression on her painting approach. Light, shape, and color add to her canvas images of a

moment captured in time; a diary of everyday life.

Stephania Dapolla
"Burano"
www.Stephmel.Etsy.com
Stephania Dapolla is a visual artist based in Athens, Greece. With a background in eastern traditional painting and academic studies in art history and philosophy, she is now devoted to artistic photography and creating nostalgic images inspired by nature, everyday poetry, urban decay, the history and light of her homeland, Greece, and the land of her origin, Italy. Fine art prints of her original photos are sold worldwide under the name "stephmel."

Carolyn Finnell
"Hide And Seek"
www.FinnellFineArt.etsy.com
Carolyn Finnell strives for an intuitive and expressive abstraction of nature and emotion. She aims to communicate attitude and personality and to establish a connection with the viewer using only color and form. Carolyn revels in the tension between order and chaos and the battle between reverence and irreverence that occurs in every piece. She paints from the inside out, always seeking the balance of deliberation and spontaneity.

Emily Jones, *Jones Design Company*
"Bushel & a Peck"
"Do Not Worry About Tomorrow"
www.JonesDesignCompany.com
Emily's love of childhood art grew into a small stationery business, which turned into a lifestyle blog. She creates original art prints, DIY projects, and delights in talking about home decorating, motherhood, blogging, and great design. Come for a visit at *www.jonesdesigncompany.com*, and hopefully you will leave encouraged and inspired.

Marianne LoMonaco
"Blackberries"
MarianneLoMonaco.Etsy.com
Marianne LoMonaco is a Toronto-born photographer. She is completely self-taught and in 2009, she finally upgraded her camera to one that actually worked. And fell in love. Hard and fast. Passionately in love. With photography. Completely driven to improve both creatively and technically, never satisfied for long without challenging herself. "It was that year I found a part of my life I was always meant to live."

Bree Madden, *Bree Madden Photography*
"Faded Memories—Ranunculus"
"Hanalei Bay"
"Golden Gate Bridge"
"Carlsbad Beach Tower"
www.BreeMadden.Etsy.com
Bree Madden is a Southern California native who has a strong passion for the beach, ocean, and photography. She likes to take inspiration from her beach living to her work and help people see what her love is all about.

Sarah B. Martinez
"Watercolor Butterflies No."
SarahBMartinez.com
After saying "goodbye" to city life and moving to the country in 2011, Sarah Martinez has brought her daydreams of becoming a flourishing artist to life. She, her musician husband, and their tiny baby moved into a magical stone house in the Northwest hills of Connecticut, where she now muses from her sunny home studio. Along with earth and sky, the flora and fauna in between are her sweetest inspirations.

Ashley Mills
"Vintage Americana—Interior"
"In Flight"
"Vintage Americana—Rest"
"Vintage Americana—Rusted"
www.thehandmadehome.net
Ashley mixes her love of art, great design, and writing into full-time fun at

Thehandmadehome.net. Here you'll find stories on a little bit of everything from the fun of parenthood to a love for everyday life.

Rachel Parker
"Silver Polish"
"Covering Ground"
"Sunday Hydrangeas"
www.RachelsStudio.com
Rachel Parker is a self-taught artist who works mainly in watercolors. As the daughter of an artist, she was raised going to painting lessons and watching her mother create. Her motivation for creation is to capture what may otherwise go unnoticed; to reveal the beauty in simple moments and objects. Making an image come alive on paper is her inspiration. Rachel has sold her work nationally and internationally through *www.rachelsstudio.com*.

David Scheirer
"8 Quail Eggs"
"Blueberries"
"Curtis Island Lighthouse"
"Lobster Buoys"
"Acorns"
"Red Lobster"
www.DSWatercolors.com
David Scheirer is a painter and illustrator living in the Washington, DC area. He works in watercolors and creates small, detailed works of art inspired by the coasts and woodlands of the eastern U.S. He enjoys bird watching, collecting fossils, beach combing, and hiking, and often comes home and paints subjects from these adventures.

Miriam Schulman
"Yasgur's Farm"
www.SchulmanArt.com
Watercolor artist Miriam Schulman is a New York native who passionately paints full-time. She is best known for her watercolor portraits, which have earned her critical recognition. She teaches her watercolor secrets online and from her New York studio. Her portraits are included in numerous private and public collections. Her paintings

have been featured in the *Art of Man*, the *New York Times*, and numerous other publications.

Michelle Tavares
"Poppies"
www.etsy.com/shop/calamaristudio
Michelle Tavares, the artist behind Calamari Studio, grew up in southern California and studied illustration and design at Utah Valley University. She now enjoys a somewhat nomadic life with her husband, Spencer, and their two sons. Michelle is most inspired by the intricacy of nature and more of her work can be seen at Etsy.com/ calamaristudio.

Amy Tyler, *Amy Tyler Photography*
"Sweet Rides"
"Torch Song"
www.AmyTylerPhotography.etsy.com
As a young adult, Amy studied fine art at Middle Tennessee State University. After spending many years as an oil pastel artist, she transitioned into photography. It was there, behind the lens of her first camera, where she truly fell in love. Amy's favorite part of photography is the post-production editing work on her computer, where her fine art background really comes into play. She loves photographing all things delicate and sweet, which led her to specialize in nursery decor.

Acknowledgments

To the amazingly talented artists who were gracious enough to share their beautiful creations with all of us: thank you. This book would not be possible without you.

To the wonderful team at Adams Media for their insight, patience, and seeing something in us, we are so humbled. You have been a delight.

And to our inspiring readers, we are forever awed and grateful for all of you.

Thank you.

About the Authors

Jamin and Ashley Mills began their adventure together as college sweethearts. After a decade of marriage and three offspring later, they currently reside with their family in Montgomery, Alabama. They are the voices behind this book and their website, *www.thehandmadehome.net*.

At The Handmade Home, they share their daily journey and down-to-earth passion as the parents to three incredible children and one crazy dog. In between the mountainous piles of dirty laundry and musical bed fiascos with their glorious little troublemakers, they're also known for their handmade revamps and one-of-a-kind projects as they create a haven for the everyday.

For more inspiring projects and one-of-a-kind creations, visit The Handmade Home at *www.thehandmadehome.net.*

Ashley *and* Jamin Mills
The Handmade Home:
Creating a Haven for the Every Day

thehand madehome .net

Bid farewell to blank walls and say hello to the art you love—all at an exceptional value.

The Custom Art Collection makes it easy and inexpensive for you to find the perfect print for every corner of your home. Featuring curated collections for contemporary, eclectic, and traditional homes, each book in this lovely series showcases original artwork from up-and-coming artists and pairs the prints with others in the collection to complete the look.

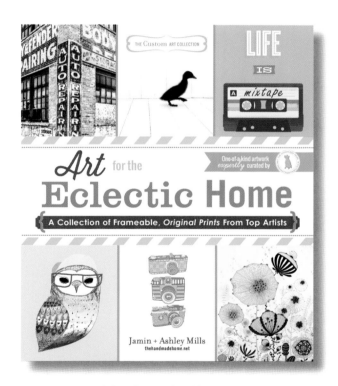

Art for the Eclectic Home
Trade Paperback
978-1-4405-7089-6, $22.99

Art for the Contemporary Home
Trade Paperback
978-1-4405-7090-6, $22.99

Beautiful DIY Décor for a One-of-a-Kind Home

Perfect for those who want to fill their space with unique personality, *Handmade Walls* offers 22 fabulous DIY projects—each easy enough to achieve in a day. Get that creative look you've always wanted without spending a fortune or succumbing to cookie-cutter designs. Your dream home design is within reach!

Handmade Walls
Trade Paperback
978-1-4405-7232-6, $24.99